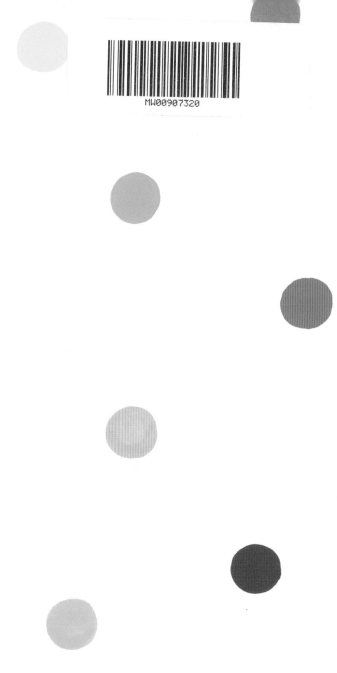

EAT, SLEEP, POOP

By Alexandra Penfold   *Illustrated by* Jane Massey

Alfred A. Knopf
New York

For Little B and Ghee, with love —A.P.

For Billy xxx —J.M.

THIS IS A BORZOI BOOK PUBLISHED BY ALFRED A. KNOPF

Text copyright © 2016 by Alexandra Penfold

Jacket art and interior illustrations copyright © 2016 by Jane Massey

All rights reserved. Published in the United States by Alfred A. Knopf,

an imprint of Random House Children's Books, a division of Penguin Random House LLC, New York.

Knopf, Borzoi Books, and the colophon are registered trademarks of Penguin Random House LLC.

Visit us on the Web! randomhousekids.com

Educators and librarians, for a variety of teaching tools, visit us at RHTeachersLibrarians.com

Library of Congress Cataloging-in-Publication Data

Names: Penfold, Alexandra, author. | Massey, Jane, author.

Title: Eat, sleep, poop / by Alexandra Penfold ; illustrated by Jane Massey.

Description: First edition. | New York : Alfred A. Knopf, [2016]

| Summary: "A humorous memoir of an infant's first few months." —Provided by publisher

Identifiers: LCCN 2015029968 | ISBN 978-0-385-75503-0 (trade) |

ISBN 978-0-385-75504-7 (lib. bdg.) | ISBN 978-0-385-75505-4 (ebook)

Subjects: | CYAC: Babies—Fiction.

Classification: LCC PZ7.1.P446 Eat 2016 | DDC [E]—dc23

LC record available at http://lccn.loc.gov/2015029968

The text of this book is set in 26-point Filosofia.

The illustrations were created using pencil and gouache.

MANUFACTURED IN MALAYSIA

November 2016

10 9 8 7 6 5 4 3 2 1

First Edition

I haven't been here very long.

But I already have a rigorous schedule.

Eat...

Sleep...

Poop!

Eat.

Sleep.

Poop.

It's a lot to fit in a single day,
but I manage.

Some days are harder than others.
And I have to cut back . . .

on the sleep.

You might say
I'm picking things up as I go.

And I think I have it
all figured out.

Eat,

sleep,

poo

ooooooop,

LOVE.